At first I was afraid,
I was petrified.

Kept thinkin' I could never live
without you by my side.

But then I spent so many nights
thinkin' how you did me wrong.

And I grew strong.
And I learned how to get along.

And so you're back
from outer space.

I just walked in to find you here
with that sad look upon your face.

I should have changed that stupid lock,
I should have made you leave your key,
if I'd have known for just one second
you'd be back to bother me.

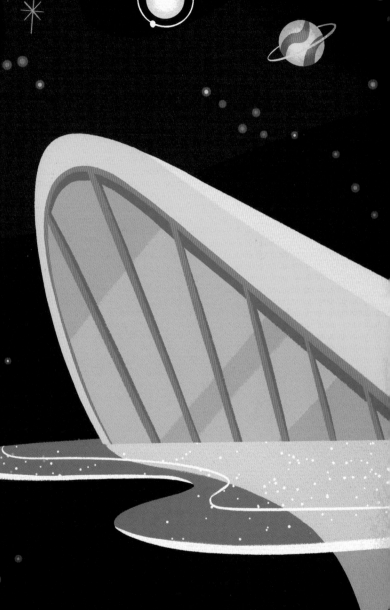

Go on now, go. Walk out the door.
Just turn around now.

'Cause you're not welcome anymore.
Weren't you the one who tried to hurt me with goodbye?

Did you think I'd crumble?
Did you think I'd lay down and die?

Oh no, not I. I will survive.
Oh, as long as I know how to love, I know I'll stay alive.

I've got all my life to live.
And I've got all my love to give, and I'll survive.

I will survive. Hey, hey.

It took all the strength I had
not to fall apart.

Kept trying hard to mend the pieces
of my broken heart.

And I spent oh so many nights
just feelin' sorry for myself.

I used to cry.
But now I hold my head up high.
And you see me.

Somebody new.
I'm not that chained-up little person
still in love with you.

And so you felt like dropping in
and just expect me to be free.

Well now I'm saving all my lovin'
for someone who's loving me.

Go on now, go. Walk out the door.
Just turn around now.

'Cause you're not welcome anymore.
Weren't you the one who tried to break me with goodbye?

Did you think I'd crumble?
Did you think I'd lay down and die?

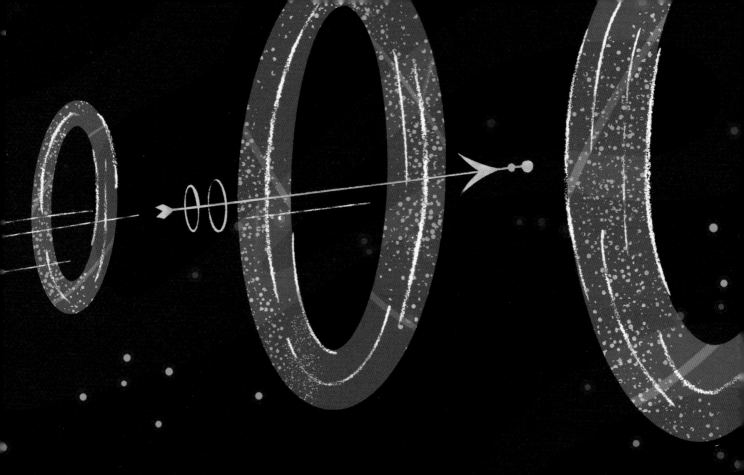

Oh no, not I. I will survive.
Oh, as long as I know how to love, I know I'll stay alive.

I've got all my life to live.
And I've got all my love to give, and I'll survive.
I will survive.

Oh . . .

Go on now, go. Walk out the door.
Just turn around now.

'Cause you're not welcome anymore.
Weren't you the one who tried to break me with goodbye?

Did you think I'd crumble?
Did you think I'd lay down and die?